Yester

By Prachatorn Joemjumroon

Copyright © Prachatorn Joemjumroon, 2022

All rights reserved. No part of this book may be reproduced in any form or by electronic or mechanical means, including information storage and retrieval systems, without permission in writing from the publisher, except by a reviewer who may quote brief passages in a review.

This is a work of fiction. Names, characters, places, and incidents either are the product of the author's imagination or are used fictitiously. Any resemblances to actual persons, living or dead, events, or locales are entirely coincidental.

ISBN 979-8369743850 (Paperback)

First Edition

Thank you to my family, friends, and everyone who supported me up to this point. I appreciate every little encouragement from all of you from the bottom of my heart.

Table Of Content

A Car's Constant Beeping	8
A Doll's Questions	10
Ancestry Anguish	12
Arrested Disturbance	14
Caillou's Callousness	16
Casino Wasteland	18
Chaotic Night	20
Cycle Of War	22
Deep End Bravery	24
Derogatory Devil	26
Dragon's Deception	28
Dreamy Escape	30
Fly, Fly Away	32
Heroic Consequences	34
Legal Apathy	36
Library Of Ideas	38

Lithuania's Lost Longing	40
Lucky Stars' Immortality	42
Machine Replacements	44
Morning Relaxation	46
Mural Painting	48
Nightmarish Pain	50
Nostalgic Dreamer	52
Now In Jail	54
Older Learners	56
Poetry Competition	58
Proudful Reader	60
Resting Time	62
Roadkill Assistance	64
Silhouettes In A Dream	66
Story Omission	68
Teriyaki Troubles	70
Timeless Ghost	72
Tough Lessons	74

Two Short Nature Poems	**76**
Wings Of An Angel	**77**
Worldwide Crossover	**79**
Ye's Offensive Attack	**81**
Yesterday's Lost Time	**83**
กรรมมีจริง*	85

Yesterday's Long Time: Poems

A Car's Constant Beeping

Outside my two-story home,
There was a car with its constant beeping,
The sensitivities to its sensors
Is that of a Venus Flytrap to its prey,
So, with any subtle movements,
A gentle breeze, a raindrop, a snowflake,
Triggers that irritating stream of noises.

I was trying to read,
Beep beep beep!
I was trying to write,
Beep beep beep!
I was trying to watch a movie,
Beep beep beep!
I was trying to sleep tonight,
Beep beep beep!

Damn it! I concede.
Beep beep beep!
I looked out my window,
Beep beep beep!
And saw the offending culprit,
Beep beep beep!
A 2017 red Toyota Prius,
Beep beep beep!

Should I go knock on their door?
Beep beep beep!
Tell them that something's wrong?
Beep beep beep!
Don't they hear it too?
Beep beep beep!
Is it also annoying them as well?
Beep beep beep!

As I was contemplating, it suddenly stopped,
Now quietness replaces the sound,
And I could finally get my deserved rest,
Be prepared for tomorrow to come,
For the challenges that lay ahead of me,
For everything in my straight path.

I awoke to the sun's rays on my face,
The birds are chirping on a branch nearby,
My alarm rang its hypnotic tones,
And I stretched my four limbs,
Removed the warm blanket from my body,
And get ready for the morning so that I -
Beep beep beep!

A Doll's Questions

A doll in an abandoned house
Asked questions I could not answer;
"Where is my creator? My benefactors?
Where is my family? Friends?
Where is the girl that held me
When lightning struck in the night,
When the monsters gave her fright,
When eating treats with such delight,
When she's saddened by her plight?
Where is she now? Is she dead?"

And as I was about to turn away,
About to run the hell out of there,
Scared for my safety, for my sanity,
She gave one final request,
A plea to a stranger like me,
Someone whom she never knew,
A desperate sound in her voice,
"Will you bring me outside?"

I lifted her off the dusty shelf,
Brushing the cobwebs and debris
Off of her ashen, plastic skin,
Trying to clean her as best I can,
But still, spots remain like a tan.

We both went out the front door,
She again sees the sun shining,
Feel the breeze from the gentle wind,
Her red, velvet hair rustles softly,
And as I set her down on the grass,
For the first in a long, forgotten time,
She seemed relieved, content,
Ready to move on once more.

And she closes her eyes,
Her body slumped over,
Not a sound out of her mouth,
No movements to write about,
Only the shell of the figurine,
Yet her wishes came true,
Her spirit entered a blissful retreat.

Ancestry Anguish

How would my ancestors see me?
See me grow up not on their soil?
See me across an ocean they can't comprehend?
See me not tilling the rice paddies?
Or not becoming a soldier for a king?
See me sitting at a desk all day,
Typing tirelessly, earning money endlessly?

Would they be happy? Angry? Saddened?
Would their ghost travel so far away,
And haunt me with lessons from the past?
Would they admonish the way I live,
Different religions, different lifestyles?
Would they be jealous of all my privileges?
Not die from diseases that plague them?
Not starve from the days of famine?
Not be bombarded from wars upon wars?

From conquerors to dictators to rulers,
Having your life be balanced in their palms,
No choice if death appears at their front door;
Would they want to switch places with me?

Instead of working under the blazing sun,
They sit on couches watching movies;
Instead of walking miles for many hours,
They travel the same distance faster now;
Instead of gambling on their child's safety,
They see them grow up protected.

Would they see me with prejudice?
Would they see me as weak? Pathetic?
Would they strip me from what I have,
Down to nothing except the clothes on,
Drop me in the middle of a jungle,
And make me survive like how they used to?
Would they wish that upon me,
And for future generations to come,
Would I have the same sentiment for them?

Arrested Disturbance

Walking on a warm autumn day,
The sun's low to the horizon,
About to rest its head once more,
Giving off the last of its rays;
Listening to my favorite J-Pop songs,
On a playlist I created for myself;
Wearing cargo shorts, a T-shirt,
And a sweater against the gentle breeze.

Halfway through my journey,
On the familiar four-way intersection,
Where cars wait their turn to pass,
Where I cross by as a pedestrian,
There was a police car parked
On the opposite side of the streets,
The man outside with his shades on,
And a woman sitting on the hood,
Handcuffs attached to her wrists,
And behind her back, a restraint,
With a blue tanktop, black tights,
And barefoot against the pavement.

For what she's arrested for I don't know,
A disturbance, a drunkard escapade,
Or something even more sinister,
And I couldn't hear what was being said,
My earphones muffled the outside.

Not my responsibility, not my problem,
So I continue on my way back home,
Not staying to see the outcome,
Wanting to get back to eat my food,
To come back to my sheltered warmth,
Where I have the luxury of that;
She's spending her time in a concrete box,
Waiting for her trial, for her punishment,
A person I'll forget in the coming days,
Until brought up in the pages of the news.

Caillou's Callousness

Caillou, that bald Canadian cartoon child,
Does what he has always been doing,
Without consequences, without persecution,
Without the wrath of God's retribution;
Parents are damned for retaliation,
Because he does not learn, no reflection,
Only crying, whining, firm altercation,
Never a chance to have a realization
Being burdensome with his chaotic actions,
But that's the price to pay for domination
Against the world's ire and vilification.

Yet, he's a mascot for a generation,
An impact on millions of those impressionable,
A teacher of some sort for them,
But instead of life lessons and the like,
To be obnoxious to get what you want.

Maybe that's what the creators aimed for,
A subversion to Sesame Streets,
Replacing role models with good morals
With an annoying brat with bad habits,
But whether intentional or not,
They created a monster for television,
An animation worthy to be shown in Hell.

Though, in the end, there was some value,
Something to take from this show,
An example, if you will, of modern life,
A small slice of behavioral realism,
Where instead of an angelic wing
Wrapping themselves around your kid,
Showing them the perfect way to live,
Respecting every and all people,
The normal, irrational demons prevail,
Causing mishaps and pain to others,
A disturbance no one appreciates,
But must endure to continue thriving,
As long as we still exist in this world,
For how long only the Divine truly knows.

Casino Wasteland

Entering the *Suquamish Clearwater Casino*
For what we came here for,
For the comedian we waited so long for,
For a distraction in the middle of the night.

But as we sat at an empty table
Near the bar, near the many games,
I felt like I do not belong in this place,
That my driver's license wasn't correct,
That the age on it wasn't real at all,
That the bouncers made a mistake,
That I am still a child at heart
Within the body of an adult.

Instead of drinking the alcohol they serve,
I had on me strawberry milk from home;
Instead of playing at the colorful slots,
With names such as *Triple Fortune Dragon Spitfire*,
I was reading *Villa Triste* by Patrick Modiano;
Instead of watching the football game,
On the wall-sized 4k HD monitor,
Lounging in the leathery chairs,
Placing bets on who would win,
I was wishing to be part of the action,
To be down there on the field,
Tackling, passing the ball, making touchdowns;
Instead of staying where we were at,
I would rather be anywhere else.

We didn't have a choice, we made our plans;
I just have to endure the noises,
The gamblings, the loss of money,
The drunks roaming the floors,
Everything that is part of the show,
Until the actual reason why we appeared,
Why we are wasting our time
Playing chess, charging our phones,
Being outsiders in this sinful dungeon,
To laugh at jokes, at the innocent fun;
The time is ticking down till then,
We are surrounded by greed and vices.

Chaotic Night

In my room, scared to move,
Crouching next to my bed,
Trying to be invisible, inconspicuous,
Clutching my pistol in my right hand,
Safety off, ready to shoot,
My mind racing a mile a minute,
This seemingly peaceful night
Suddenly turned into a chaotic mess.

Beyond my walls, the neighbors,
Banging away on many objects,
Making a ruckus in a frequent matter,
As loud as thunderbolts,
As frightening as the unknown.

Beyond my windows, the iconic sight,
The red and blue flashing lights,
Alternatively pulsing in a rhythmic fashion,
Like blood flowing in veins and arteries,
The siren noise envelops the place,
A blanket to cover both my ears,
No other sounds dare to pierce.

Don't know what's going on,
Don't know what's happening,
All I see is the space around me,
Within the prison of my own home,
Within a box to hide from the demons.

Trying to close my eyes, to sleep,
To have time pass by faster than ever,
To make this just a nightmare,
And not a real scene in the real world,
But my body rejects slumberness,
Embracing heightened emotions,
Invisible caffeine flowing through me,
Constant internal dopamine injections,
And I can only wait for it to end,
On a small, wooden, hastily-made dinghy
Hoping that these will be gentle waves,
Instead of massive, destructive tsunamis.

Cycle Of War

One man. One decision.
A speech was made in the afternoon.
A push of a few buttons.
An enemy has been established.

Hundreds of thousands called to arms.
Boys are about to be turned into men.
Girls are about to be turned into women.
Volunteered and indentured mixed in.
Guns purchased in the millions.
Armor of various sizes fitted.
Vehicles with the newest technology.
All were trained to shoot and kill.

The battle started. The war has begun.
Bang! Bang! Boom! Boom!
Bullets flew across the fields
Like flies moving in a blink of an eye.
Shouts of abuse and pain exploded.
Bodies faced down in the mud.
Limbs and blood spread out.
A casualty a couple of seconds,
Whoever has a less death toll
Wins the match for dominance.

Soldiers become veterans.
Crutches and slings in abundance.
Families hoped for the best,
Or mourning for their losses.
Stories shared around the dinner tables,
To preserve, to not be forgotten.

Those at the top of the food chain,
Discuss amongst one another,
Allies and opponents alike.
Meals prepped by world-renowned chefs,
Without lifting a finger,
Without pulling a trigger,
Diplomacy at the very tip of a hill
From the muscles of the commonwealth.
A decision was reached. Peace achieved.
Then a disagreement comes into play.
Everything resets at the end of the day.

Deep End Bravery

A tennis ball in the deep end,
And as a seven-year-old,
I did not know how to swim,
But that did not deter me,
Did not back me down from the challenge
And accept the loss and walk away.

Was it bravery? Stupidity? I don't know.
But with the only clothes I had on,
I jumped in the pool without hesitation,
Without a second thought for my safety,
And doggy paddle towards it,
And doggy paddle back to land,
All within a few minutes at most,
Though it felt like hours had passed.

For a while, I was shivering,
Everything I wore was soaked,
Sitting on the concrete pavement,
Basking under the blazing rays of the sun,
Waiting for the Dry Spell to take effect.

I reflected on what had transpired,
What had happened the moments prior,
And I laughed aloud to myself,
At what a fool I had become,
To risk my life for a cheap toy,
Something that's replaceable,
Though in the end, it was worth it,
Not for the product in the end,
But for the journey, the adventure,
The development of my character,
The boost in integrity and vitality.

And I got up feeling relieved,
Ready to head home for comfort,
Ready to face the problems onward,
Not as the person I once was before,
But a new one moving slightly forward.

Derogatory Devil

I shouldn't call a fat person fat.
I shouldn't call a short person short.
I shouldn't use derogatory slurs.
I shouldn't exhibit any speeches of hate.

I know that. I really do.
But why do they exist in my mind?
Why do they want to escape from my mouth?
Why is there an urge to utter them
In private, or, God forbid, to someone's face?
Am I racist, sexist, homophobic?
Is this my true character,
And the me outside a facade?

I try to be polite to everyone I meet,
But there's a devil whispering in my ear,
Tempting me to say the worse,
Enticing me to be a bully to others,
Wanting the world to suffer,
And me to be an arbiter in disguise.

I continue to fight off this side,
This entity that's growing in power
And sometimes I weaken a little,
Whether through tiredness or whatnot,
My blade is getting duller and more rigid,
And I have to sharpen it every time.

But that energy needs to be recharged,
And in between each session,
The dark forces envelop further,
Until it's time to release the beast.

Though luckily, I am alone
To once again push back this demon
To its chambers where it sleeps,
Where this never-ending cycle
Renews itself for a future battle.

Dragon's Deception

The dragon, all mighty and fierce,
Looked down at her next opponent,
A squire, all scrawny and weak,
Holding not a sword like Excaliber,
But a dingy, pathetic dagger,
That could not pierce the hide of a cattle.

Trying to stomp him to the ground,
To finish the fight with such ease,
Before going back to her dinner,
But he was nimble, he was fast,
He was like an annoying fly,
He dodges the powerful foot.

Claws sharpened and teeth bared,
Biting and scratching at the insect,
Yet he hid behind rocks, behind walls,
In holes she could not reach.

At last, she had enough of the game,
Enough of the humiliation she endured,
And with a long-drawn breath,
She exhaled a massive stream of fire,
Engulfing the ground with an inferno flare,
The shape of the flame is like a spire
The radiance is strong like the sun's glare.

And once the scorched earth simmered,
Once the ashes were blown by the wind,
She was surprised by what she saw,
Standing at the cave's entrance
Was the boy all triumph-looking,
With a small, shiny chalice in his hand,
Because when she was blinded by her rage,
He hid behind her coveted spot,
Her mountain of golden trinkets,
Grabbed just a small treasure,
And when the smoke hid all visions,
Ran like hell towards freedom,
Towards his master's embrace.

And she laughed to herself,
Let him run off with his reward;
Instead of strength being the victor,
Cunning was lurking in the shadows,
Ready to strike when least expected.

Dreamy Escape

The less I sleep, the more I dream,
Replacing the long, dark void
For an adventure, for an expedition,
For an excuse to live in a fantasy,
Instead of facing the truth of it all.

Forget logic, forget limitations,
Forget everything that's weighing me down,
And go fly through the endless sky,
Or be in my own short film for once,
Be the protagonist that I wanted to be,
Or connect with people from the past,
Those who are no longer near me,
Whether dead or alive I do not know,
Whether they remember me I do not know,
Whether they are happy I do not know.

When the sun's gone, a distraction is needed,
When thoughts are tormenting me,
A little escape is sometimes needed,
To run away to, to flee from the shine
And retreat back to my safe space,
Back where monsters cannot hurt me,
Cannot penetrate my vulnerability,
Cannot destroy what I hold dear.

But I open my eyes, and everything's gone,
The light shone through the windows,
Hitting where my castle is located,
Breaking down the walls, brick by brick,
Like mini cannon balls from a trebuchet,
Or bullets from a high-powered rifle,
The shield's disintegrating, dissolving,
And I have to wake up, to live on,
Until it regenerates, rebuilds itself,
And I start right back to the very start,
An endless cycle to the finish line,
Where one last dream lasts for eternity.

Fly, Fly Away

Fly, fly away to Neverland.
Fly, fly away with Tinkle Bell.
Fly, fly away from Captain Hook.
Fly, fly away; goodbye, goodbye.

Arguing Parents; fly, fly away.
Demanding teachers; fly, fly away.
Monitoring molesters; fly, fly away.
Fly, fly away; goodbye, goodbye.

Loneliness; fly, fly away.
Isolation; fly, fly away.
Perverted mind; fly, fly away.
Tormenting thoughts; fly, fly away.
Fly, fly away; goodbye, goodbye.

Remove my shackles and I'll fly, fly away.
Remove my blindfold and I'll fly, fly away.
Remove my cage and I'll fly, fly away.
Remove my sanctuary and I'll fly, fly away.
Remove me from you and I'll fly, fly away.
Fly, fly away; goodbye, goodbye.

Close to the sun; fly, fly away.
Close to Heaven; fly, fly away.
Close to Hell; fly, fly away.
Close to what's between; fly, fly away.
Fly, fly away; goodbye, goodbye.

It's time to spread my winds
And soar in the open sky;
It's time to leave the ground,
And be alongside the angels;
It's time to touch the clouds,
Instead of the dirt beneath;
It's time, my son, to go,
And leave you to your own path;
Fly, fly away; goodbye, goodbye.

Heroic Consequences

The villain is vanquished, the day is saved,
The hero swings away feeling contented,
Or flew away to neighboring cities,
Ready for the next time they're needed,
The crowd cheering them on,
Relieved of the evil presently known,
Newscasters reporting the events prior,
All's well that end's well…right?

Those involved can freely go,
Or within the walls of a prison cell,
While the common citizen, the average Joe,
Have to foot the bill for their actions,
Have to clean up after themselves,
Like janitors for all the rowdy students.

Cars destroyed, work in jeopardy;
Homes demolished, nowhere to sleep;
Communities devastated, families weep;
Bodies lost, loved ones mourn softly;
Battles ended, yet consequences reigned.

Do they even care about us?
Are they too absorbed in being in the spotlight?
Too selfish as the protagonist
That the shadowed characters
Are seen as unfortunate collateral?

Restoration is not in their self-made contracts,
Only being a knight, slaying the dragon
And rescuing the princess and her people,
Not to rebuild, brick by brick,
A job for the impoverished, lowly humans,
A task unworthy of their polished hands,
And as they continued on their countless crusades,
We are the ants overlooked from above.

Legal Apathy

The prosecution wants me in jail,
The defendant is doing his job,
The jury is listening intently,
The judge is there to moderate,
And I'm sitting in my wooden chair,
Staring into space, into the void,
Not caring about the procedure,
Not noticing the arguments on both sides,
Just lost in my own mind,
Thinking about the breakfast I ate,
Thinking about the episode I watched,
Thinking about how hot my shower was,
Thinking about the events before this.

If I'm thrown in prison, then so be it.
If I'm released today, then so be it.
I have no plans for what comes next,
Letting the flow of time get to me,
The lights are on, but no one's home,
All I need is to be alone right now,
Whether in a cell or in my room doesn't matter,
I want to be away from this circus show,
Away from the continuous talking,
Away from all of this, from the public,
Locking me up and discarding the key,
That's all I desire, all I ever wanted.

But before I get what I wished for,
I have to endure this charade,
To keep quiet and hear the noises,
Back and forth, back and forth,
The lawyers are performing passionately,
While the center character is apathetic,
Counting down the minutes on the clock.

As the session is about to be over,
I am escorted out of the court,
My shackles clanged against each other,
Waiting for the next day to arrive,
To announce the verdict of my judgment,
All the while, under the nightly sky,
I am in solitude, no one's bothering me,
And I slept peacefully on my cotton bed.

Library Of Ideas

Every thought from every person
Coalesce into a single library,
Where the rows of shelves,
Containing millions each day,
Continues to grow, prosper,
With no end in sight, no finish line,
Just stretching far the eye could see
And further beyond well into the darkness,
And the higher it goes, the closer it becomes
To reach where the angels reside in.

Everyone will fail, though some have tried,
Reading each of them one at a time,
From beginning to end with stops in between,
Until they understood anything and everything
But their strong endeavor seems pointless,
As with the completion of one
Adds another or two to the long list,
Though their determination is admirable,
They should at least be rewarded with that.

While they spend their time wasting away
In a comfy leather chair next to the fire,
With a book in hand, absorbing its contents,
And a pile nearby rising towards the birds,
I, and many others, are going to exist,
To live our lives the best as we can,
To enjoy what little light we have left,
Until we eventually join with the abyss,
And with each passing day and night,
As we are lost in thought at our desks,
Or get comfy in a dreamy state,
We are gradually increasing the size,
Ballooning the collection in the room,
So that those that are there are ready
To feed their eternal void of a stomach,
To satiate their desire for knowledge,
Stationed to forever learn with no goal in mind.

Lithuania's Lost Longing

Lithuania, like a lost lover,
I yearned for your touch,
To walk on your soil,
Meet your people, eat your food,
Visit places where legends once stood.

I had a chance to embrace you,
To stay for the first time,
Away from friends, away from family,
Just me into your unknown grasps.

I made my passport, made my money,
Made connections along the way,
Like Romeo to his Juliet,
I was mere moments from contact,
Only time was a factor before,
The clock ticking down the minutes.

But alas, in the end, I could not,
Like the star-struck couple
During their fatalities in the fifth act,
We were barred to come together,
To see all that you contain,
The best and the worst of you,
The light extinguished our encounter.

The overlords deemed it not so,
The sickness that plagued the world,
The unforeseen events occurring,
I had to be confined to where I'm at,
Seeing you at a far distance,
Like being stuck on an island with no boat,
No ship to cross the vast ocean.

But maybe in the future,
I might be a guest again,
Be invited to join your abode,
Be a wandering traveler
And stumble into your place,
How I hope that would be so,
The omnipotent can uniquely tell.

Lucky Stars' Immortality

Watched *Lucky Stars* in seventh grade,
Where someone who's inexperienced
Looking at those in their senior year of high school,
Doing activities I would be doing later on,
Making jokes, playing games, having fun,
Having more freedom than I ever had
Something I was in anticipation of.

Years later, I have now finished college,
I am wiser, more informed,
Instead of the pathetic mustache I had prior,
A full beard covers my lower head,
The world's opened more so than before.

Yet, the four girls are still the same,
No growth, no change, nothing,
They're still the age from long past,
Did not even finish secondary schooling,
And I looked at them with sadness,
They're at the mercy of their creators,
Cannot develop without their consent,
Cannot continue for a normal length of time,
Being stuck reliving the moments,
Like stranded within an endless cycle,
No way to escape, no way to move on.

Lost friends I haven't seen in a while,
I was naive, incompetent, inept,
I looked to you all for some escape;
In the present, though, I am older,
Looking behind them instead of forward,
As you all are trapped within your bubble,
And I am walking away every day,
Becoming just a passing memory,
Until someone out there relinquishes,
And create a sequel of all your futures.

Machine Replacements

A reoccurring thought comes to mind,
When I lay my head to rest on my bed,
Of how obsolete we're making ourselves be
With each and every technological achievement.

Steel replacing flesh.
Metal replacing bones.
Electricity replacing blood.
Circuitry replacing veins.
Predicted algorithms replacing chaotic ideas.
Augmentations replacing weaknesses.
Temporary damages replacing permanent injuries.

We are becoming second-tier,
A rank below the very top,
And we cannot fault anyone but our own,
Our curiosity will become our doom,
The pursuit of a better future,
Will be detrimental to the present,
And we will become the people of the past.

We will turn into the people of *Wall-E*,
Apathetic, disabled, overweight,
If we continue to fly too close to the sun,
Continue to tread on unknown territory,
Without recourse, without backup plans,
Moving forward with blinding speed,
No mention of the upcoming consequences.

I can shout out my concerns,
But I feel I will be heard on deaf ears,
Because regardless of the ramifications,
There are those who will open Pandora's Box,
Forcibly squeeze the paste out of the tube,
Even with blaring warning signs overhead,
Ignoring what we should all fear the most,
Being forgotten by our created designs.

Morning Relaxation

Under the bright, morning sun,
The grass was covered with dew,
The nightly fire turned to ash,
The other campers are up and about,
And I'm sitting on the chair,
Looking out towards the scenery,
With *When We Were Orphans* in hand,
And a notebook and pencil at my side.

My friends were out for exciting matters,
Diving, jumping into the "Devil's Punchbowl,"
And they asked me to join them,
To relish this moment of our trip,
But I refused, wasn't feeling it,
With straight days prior to adventure,
I wanted to use this time to wind down,
To take a sort of breather, to relax,
Like a slow jog in the middle of a marathon,
To conserve my energy for more to come,
And they agreed to my proposition,
Not deterred by their relenting temptation,
And left me on my own meditation.

I got in a few pages completed,
Finished the prologue, learned the characters,
Waiting for them to return,
Wating to pack up and be our way,
Cleaning myself at the communal showers,
Eating breakfast, drinking black coffee
In the main dining room hall,
Charging my phone at a nearby outlet,
Getting back to the story for another round.

Closer to an hour later, they came back,
All drenched and shivering,
Towels draped over themselves,
And I greeted them my usual way,
As they dried and put on clean clothes.

I put away some stuff in the car,
Ready to put our gears in motion,
To be on the road to liberation,
To move on to our next destination,
The clock is ticking for exploration.

Mural Painting

I saw the full mural painting
That a Michigan high school student drew,
And it did what it was expected to do,
Bringing smiles to the children at the hospital,
A pool of positivity in a sea of negativity,
Nothing more, nothing less, just ordinary.

But these parents, they saw something else,
Saw the demons emanating out of it,
Saw Satan exuding his presence,
Saw Beezlebub influencing the younger generation,
Calling the creator a worshiper of the Dark Lord,
Like the people at the Salam witch trials,
Making her cry out in pain, in disgust,
That the adults would think they are heroes,
Bullying her for their own insecurities,
Stripping the joy she had on her project
Because they felt threatened, offended,
Their children none the wiser
Of how evil their supposed protectors are acting.

Was the Christian faith used as a front?
Was there more to this than what it seemed?
Boredom? Entitlement? Propaganda?
What made them attack someone
Decades younger with vitriol words,
With insidious imagery and harsh demands?
Why, oh why they are all like this?

The herd mentality is strong in this town,
A community supported by spiteful hate,
A foundation that continues to be strong
As they absorb what they always hear,
Whether real or not has no relevance,
Whatever justifies their own beliefs
Is the only push for them to fight on,
Only a breeze of a gentle wind
To shut down what rational thoughts they have,
But on the bright side in this dark room,
At least they are together on something,
Though I wish it would have been for good,
And not for the devils they rally against.

Nightmarish Pain

Woke up in the middle of the night,
Shivering, shaking like a rattle,
My internal temperature dropped drastically,
Feeling like being in the Russian tundras
Instead of sleeping on my lofty bed
With the heater doing its work
Defending against the winter breeze.

My stomach growled and rumbled,
Like I haven't eaten the dinner I had,
But my throat and my mind are at odds,
With one with instinct urges to throw up,
And the other fighting to hold it back.

I can only twist and turn in place,
From side to side with some difficulty;
My legs were weak to stand me up;
I tried to speak, but nothing came,
Like my vocal cords had been cut;
My eyes are in rapid motion,
Doing diagonals during the brief interval,
Looking at all the ceiling's corners,
But no answer will ever come from them;
I am stuck within my own body,
A prisoner where the key disappeared,
Isolated with no help to be seen,
Replaying memories of the past,
A mechanism for distraction.

Finally, after minutes of torture,
I close the lids and drifted to sleep,
No dreams, no fantasy retellings,
Just blackness for time to pass by.

Hours later, I woke up like normal,
The sun hiding behind the foreboding clouds,
And I felt I reverted to my original self,
No harm, no discomforts, no pain,
Squeezing and opening my hands at ease,
Stretching my limbs, joints popping,
And I questioned whether that was real,
Or was it a nightmare haunting my fears?

Nostalgic Dreamer

I woke up with a start.
I felt ice set in my heart.
A dream that I just had.
A dream that I went mad.
A dream that I don't remember,
In the middle of a night in November.
This dream seemed so real,
Like a celebrity with their appeal,
But pull back the layers of dirt,
I sat there, staring, sluggish, inert.
What I once truly believed in,
Might be created by the makers of sin,
Might be conceived by their imaginations,
As I lay there, frozen by the anticipations,
Trying to fool me with trickery,
Trying to trap me in mockery,
Shine the light, making me blind,
Crumble within my own mind.
I try to forget, to go back to sleep
To go back to the time I held deep,
But I cannot rewind to Paradise,
Cannot escape my biggest vice.
I am barred from my own sanctuary,
Being hunted by an internal mercenary.

So, I have a choice between diverging roads;
One to succumb to my own demonic toads,
Or to continue moving forward, never looking back,
Never revert to a place without that crack.
And I did such that, become a drifter,
To wander away, to survive, to pilfer,
Until I found that special something,
That trophy that I'm yearning to bring,
So that I could spread both my wings,
And fly away to Heaven's hypnotic ping.
But when that is finally reached,
That steel wall beginning to be breached,
I'll just roam the desert planes,
Lost, shackled by these heavy chains,
Looking onward with no end in sight,
The tunnel shields me from the angelic light.

Now In Jail

Had sex with my unmarried lover in Bali,
And now I am in jail.
Played *Pokémon Go* in a Moscow Church,
And now I am in jail.
Chewed gum outside in Singapore,
And now I am in jail.
Ran out of gas on the German Autobahn,
And now I am in jail.
Fed hungry pigeons in Venice,
And now I am in jail.
Forgot my wife's birthday in Samoa,
And now I am in jail.
Wore a *Winnie the Pooh* shirt in Poland,
And now I am in jail.
Wore a mask on the streets in Denmark,
And now I am in jail.
Took a selfie with a Buddha statue in Sri Lanka,
And now I am in jail.
Flown a kite in the air in Victoria, Australia,
And now I am in jail.

Swore in the United Arab Emirates,
And now I am in jail.
Didn't walk my dogs every day in Rome,
And now I am in jail.
Built a sandcastle in Spain,
And now I am in jail.
Reincarnated without permission in China,
And now I am in jail.
Climbed a mighty tree in Toronto,
And now I am in jail.
Stopped by the police in the United States,
And now I am buried in the ground.

Older Learners

More respect for those in their sunset years
When they are close to retirement,
When they see their children become adults,
When their story is almost completed
And only a few pages are left to be written,
To go back to learn, to educate themselves
To become better than they once were,
Than those who just started living,
Who completed their prologue,
Who's about to experience the world,
Who are coerced to continue in school,
Forced by social pressures to do so,
The desired expectations they have to endure.

These people are told what to undertake,
And not in total control of their actions,
While men and women of the past,
Understanding the generation of the present,
And helping to improve for the future,
I give my undying support for,
Because there is no urgency, no rush,
No sense of a hidden, ulterior motive,
Becoming scholars for the sake of it.

To me, that's admirable, courageous,
That's the reason I tip my hat to them,
And why I want to follow in their footsteps
Once I am at that age, my bones are creaking,
And my importance seems to simmer down,
Gathering up the resources for this luxury,
Hitting the books on various subjects,
Be both a student to current instructors,
And a teacher to those still developing,
But I'll have to wait for a long time,
And until then, I need to work hard
To live that kind of life I wanted for myself.

Poetry Competition

A competition by a local library
To write a haiku or a tweet-long poem
About nature, about trees,
About flowers blooming under the blazing sun,
About anything organic and nonhuman.

It should be easy. It should be fast.
It should just be a straightforward task.
A grade-school-level difficulty,
Something that should be a piece of cake.

Yet days, weeks pass on by,
And nothing concrete comes to mind,
Though fragments here and there,
Like having an assortment of jigsaw puzzles,
But not enough to make a complete picture.

Why? I continually ask myself.
Why can't I write three lines?
Can't write 200 words or less?
Can't give them the bare minimum
To easily please the judges
And win the prize of publication?
Why is this giving me such a headache?

Maybe the simplicity is the challenge,
To condense thought-provoking ideas
Into something a child would understand,
Like teaching the causes of the Civil War
Through Tik-Tok videos and dancing,
Or maybe I just don't have the heart for it,
Not interesting, not fulfilling,
Like an assignment for school
And not something I put much passion in.

Though as I ponder the real reason
The computer screen is still blank,
The pages in my notebook are unwritten,
The clock is ticking, nights continue,
The deadline looms over my head,
And I'm left with agony from disbelief.

Proudful Reader

Just finished *Heart of the Night* by Naguib Mahfouz
At the wooden table in my local library,
And I want to talk about the book,
To have a chat about the novella,
To share my thoughts about the story,
To give out my immediate opinions,
To have someone to be there and listen.

But there was no one who would want to,
No one who would lend me their ear,
No one batted an eye in my direction,
And instead, are busy with themselves,
On their computers doing their work,
Looking at the rows of books on the shelf,
Minding their own business, ignoring me.

And I just sat there with pent-up energy,
Wanting to have just a small conversation,
And with my options already limited,
I went to the one person in this place,
The one person who gets paid to sit there
And listen to the patrons and their problems,
Always have free time at their disposal,
Since few people showed up at this hour,
So I thought I had a sort of chance,
A bucket to speak my mind into;
I was ready to make that pivotal step.

But she was preoccupied, unavailable,
Conversing with their co-workers,
About what I did not truly know,
And so I waited for them to conclude,
Browsing the selections they have
From authors that are well-known,
To ones that are lost in obscurity,
Biding my time for them to be free,
But they would not stop,
They have all the time in the world,
And decided to use it without me.

After a few, long, awkward minutes,
Staring back towards them at a distance
Like a stalker observing their prey in their home,
They were still deep in their discussion,
And I had to cut my losses short,
Moving on, leaving the establishment,
Entering the cold, winter air,
The temperature dropped below zero,
My teeth were chattering,
My skin was dry and flakey,
My fingers and toes were numb.

When I entered my car, turned on the heater,
Drove off back to where I live,
I thought that I had important significance,
But I was only a small side character,
Not even making a dent in that day's history.

Resting Time

Finishing the last pages of *Watermark*
At one of the cubicles in Suzzallo,
On the second floor far in the back,
Hidden between "UA" and "WZ",
Next to a huge window overlooking
The walkway where students pass by.

Though on a Sunday afternoon,
Everyone's resting after partying,
Or praying to the Lord and Savior,
Leaving the place almost empty,
A few wandering souls out and about,
Studying the materials from classes,
Or browsing the Internet wasting time.

It's peaceful, no one being a bother,
No distractions, no loud disturbances,
Silent beside the electric overhead fan,
I'm left to my own devices,
Left to do whatever I legally can.

The clock is ticking, yet I'm in no rush,
No plans scheduled for the next few hours,
No calls to answer, no texts to reply to,
Only worry about what food to eat,
A relaxation period that I divulge in.

Afterward, I started a Dean Koontz's novel,
The sun now touching the horizon,
Where before, the sky was light blue,
Now an assortment of red and purple,
The shadows are longer, skinnier,
Stretched out like an accordion.

Finally, the transition to the moon,
The colors faded into the black void,
The dark consumes all once again,
And I couldn't see what was outside,
Couldn't see the finest details.

This is now the time for me to leave,
To say goodbye to the quietness,
And off to join back into society,
To come back to the routine life I lead,
Until one day, when everything's done,
I return to enjoy what I truly desire.

Roadkill Assistance

A murder of crows surrounds roadkill,
Without any challenges, without a skill,
Waiting for the stupid animal
To wander onto oncoming traffic,
Where the bipedal masterminds
With their machinery of all kinds,
Unaware outside their field of vision,
Squash the beast with great precision,
Like God's judgment with a quick decision,
The mess on the road, natural selection.

Now the festivities have begun,
Feasting on its innards, on its flesh,
On the skin of the dead so fresh,
Pecking, getting as much as they can,
A free-for-all for an unexpected plan,
A surprise hotpot to fill their stomach,
Until the next time this happens again.

And the person who did the crime,
The accomplice for their happy meal,
Probably think it wasn't worth their time,
Wasn't worth going back and feel
Any sadness or burden to themselves,
And continue on their way without remorse,
A momentary setback on their routine course,
A few seconds event not to worry about,
No important memory to ever recount,
Just a daily excursion, a drop in a bucket,
No reason to whine, no reason to cry,
A normal day like hanging laundry to dry.

But months, years of growth wasted,
The family of the deceased mourned,
Expecting for them to return, to come back,
The food they collect for an afternoon snack,
Hoping for the best for their loved one,
But left basking under the setting sun,
Wishing that things were differently done,
One journey ends while another continues on.

Silhouettes In A Dream

Sitting on the edge of my bed,
Both hands rubbing my face,
Eyes adjusting themselves to the darkness,
Sweat poured out of my skin,
The little hairs standing upright,
And I'm left confused and frightened.

That was a nightmare, or was it?
It felt like one, sounded like one,
And I'm awake in my own room,
So, it should be just a dream.

Yet, why did it seem so real?
So vivid, like I was actually there,
Running in an endless corridor,
Away from the dark silhouettes,
Away from the many shadows,
Where did they take me to?

It's the middle of the night,
And I should go back to sleep,
Go back to my slumbering state,
And worry about this in the morning.

But I am now on full alert,
My body refused to relax,
Refused to loosen itself,
Instead, become frigid and stiff as a board,
My heartbeat getting faster and faster,
And I couldn't be calm as I once was,
My focus is on every smallest detail,
From corners to walls to the ceiling fan,
And I am trapped where I lay.

With my attention being ever so sensitive,
I heard the faintest noise,
Like whisperings of a small child,
And then creaking from the door,
Whether the wind is to blame I don't know,
This torment kept me in terror,
Until I could see the peeking
Of the rising sun of the early hours.

Story Omission

Lunch at *The Cheesecake Factory*
With a friend from college,
Seating on opposite sides of the table,
Reading the fancy, laminated menu,
Ordering pasta with bacon toppings,
Alongside breadsticks with butter.

While waiting, we have our conversations,
Discussions to pass the time,
Topics we normally already have,
Sometimes boring, sometimes interesting,
And sometimes new and exciting.

Our food came, and we started eating,
And in the middle of the meal,
Slurping noodles into our mouths,
I asked for his permission,
His blessings for an event he witnessed,
Content that is both common in nature,
And unique in a piece of literature.

He declined, and I reluctantly agreed,
Though my writing urge wants me to,
To put on paper this story to tell,
But he has his privacy, his dignity,
His reasons for keeping it hidden,
And I will respect his wishes;
Maybe future endeavors will say otherwise.

We finish what we ordered,
Paid separately what we got,
Thanked our waiter for his job,
And left the establishment fulfilled,
Though for my stomach and not my mind.

Teriyaki Troubles

In line at *BB Teriyaki*,
About to order what I want to eat,
Where the man ahead, a complete stranger,
Asked me to pay for his meal.

I was stunned. I was perplexed.
I was as confused as any person would,
And I was speechless for a second,
Trying to process what was said,
Trying to understand the situation.

When I comprehended his request,
I gave him a resounding no,
That I'm also struggling like him,
Though at differing levels I admit,
And I'm not a charity handing out money,
I don't have the luxury to share my wealth,
Don't have the security to do so.

But he keeps on persisting,
Giving me his countless pleas,
That he will go hungry for the night,
That he hadn't eaten for many hours,
Trying to win my sympathy,
Trying to get free food in the end.

But I stood my ground, stood erect,
Insistent on my refusal to his begging,
And he gave me a look of sadness,
Like betraying a comrade in war,
Using what he has to guilt me,
Using what he knows as a weapon,
And the employee was dumbstruck,
His dish had already been prepared,
Ready to hand him the finished product,
Waiting for the transaction to be made.

After minutes of his attack,
He finally left the establishment,
Without nourishment, without anything,
Going into the cold breeze empty-handed,
And I felt horrible for doing nothing,
But I need to look after myself,
Before caring for others around.

Timeless Ghost

A ghost wanders out of time,
His killer met his untimely demise,
Everyone he knew moved on,
Generations upon generations transpired,
Yet he still roams under the blazing sun.

Instead of the small village he grew up in,
Now it's a bustling metropolis;
Instead of horse-drawn carriages,
Now it's machines powered on gasoline;
Instead of only birds occupying the skies,
Now there are joined with metal imitations;
Instead of communicating face-to-face,
Now there are magic boxes they speak into.

"I am a stranger. I do not belong here.
I already forgave him. I am relieved.
My anger, though it still lingers, subsided.
So, why am I trapped in this world,
Looking on just as a spectator,
While he gets to be on the other side,
On a realm welcoming of his kind,
And I'm a lonely soul with a forgotten past."

But his cries were unanswered,
His torments continue,
His pleas are heard by deaf ears,
And he is left in perpetual pain,
The Divine playing a disturbing prank,
Or are they teaching a lesson of sorts?
Some moral he needs to find out?
Some tasks that he needs to do?
What is it? Why is he here?
Where is his guidance? His mentor?
His ferryman for the River of Styx?

Today, he waits for a sounding call.
Tomorrow, a week, a hundred years,
He will do the same as the day before,
Patient, with no sense of urgency,
Learning the different breeds of people,
Observing their many different habits,
Understanding them not of his own,
Until the eventual judgmental hand
Finally picks him up from below,
Reuniting himself with his loving wife,
And his sons, much older than he was previously.

Tough Lessons

Reading *Tarzan of the Apes*,
In the library on a Saturday afternoon,
Where behind, a mother, I assume,
Was teaching her child basic arithmetics.

But she was ruthless, she was cruel,
She was the ugly stepmother,
While her little Cinderella suffers,
As when she made some small mistakes,
Her reprimands seem too tough,
Too aggressive if you ask me,
Too much for anyone at that age.

Instead of being Kala, a lovely being,
She was Tublat, ready to punish,
Ready to destroy their innocence,
And show them the brutal wilderness.

I sympathized with the young person,
Her fight or flight is off the charts,
Wanting to escape, wanting to flee,
Wanting to be anywhere but there,
Away from the monster that God gave her,
And enjoy what time she has left.

But she cannot, stationed to her chair,
Glued to the harsh words of the adult,
Her pleading cries met with disdain,
Her distracted mind is her way out,
Her sanctuary to the jungle outside,
Waiting for Sabor to leave her alone,
But alas, she is always within her grasp,
And I am just one of the monkeys,
One of the side animals within the story,
Making no impact throughout her journey.

Two Short Nature Poems

The Cycle Of Trees

Seeds will become trees.
Seasons pass; storms are coming.
Fallen, yet reborn.

Orchestra Of Nature

Birds are chirping, bees are buzzing,
The gentle breeze is whistling;
Frogs are croaking, dogs are barking,
The leaves of many trees are rattling;
Owls are hooting, wolves are howling,
The orchestra of nature is now playing.

Wings Of An Angel

The neighbor's dog that greets me
Whenever I walk out of my porch
Did not show up one afternoon;
I asked the owners about it,
And they responded:
"Off to be in the wings of an angel."

The cat living in the alleyway
Where I feed her a can of tuna
As I pass by to and from work
Was sick and feeble and delirious;
Rushed to the veterinarian,
With her in my arms, shaking;
I waited to hear the results,
They came out and said to me:
"Off to be in the wings of an angel."

I had an argument with my lover,
They got their wallet, their car keys,
And drove out into the night;
The next morning I heard the news
How there seemed to be an accident;
The finals words I heard from them
As I turned off the television was:
"Off to be in the wings of an angel."

I visit my grandma at the hospital,
Flowers in my right hand,
A book to read to her in my left,
And after a couple of hours together,
I went home to repeat the cycle again;
I got a sudden call one night,
The doctor informed me outright,
Telling to come, to sign some papers;
At the other end of the line,
I heard a faint whisper before hanging up:
"Off to be in the wings of an angel."

I see my lifeless body on the floor,
The overflow of cocaine in my body,
And the rest scattered across galore;
Floating high to the ceiling I go,
Looking down below, down to the earth,
But up to the sky, I see the light,
The glow beckoning me to follow,
And I did so with no hesitation;
A prayer to myself one last time:
"Off to be in the wings of an angel."

Worldwide Crossover

Should there be an anime of *Huckleberry Finn*,
A Japanese interpretation of this American tale?
Should there be a French film of *No-No Boy*?
A German's *Grapes of Wrath*?
A Chinese's *Call of the Wild*?
Should there be international versions
Of stories specific to a region of the world?
Should there, or should there be not?

I would like to see how they see them,
How an outsider portrays the seriousness
And the sensitivities that they contain,
How an event hundreds of miles away
Could influence the strangers looking in,
How different beliefs clash with each other.

Would they mess up? A wrong approach?
I hope not, but you never know.
Is this cultural appropriation? An insult?
Unless they're incompetent or ignorant,
But I would only know if they make them.

The US made its own *Les Misérables*,
Their own Hollywood *Silence*,
The Disney animation of *Mulan*,
So why couldn't they do the same
Their take on our best works,
Or is that too much to ask?

Are we guarded about ourselves,
A critical eye before development,
No chances to butcher the acclaimed,
Deliver not the nuances and issues,
But a joke, a clown's performance,
A way to laugh about our history,
Our problems throughout time,
And not sympathize with our pain,
Our suffering in our weakened states,
Though that's the risk I would endure
For a chance to unite the people
From all the corners under one umbrella.

Ye's Offensive Attack

While I was reading "Miss Vincent,"
I've been listening to Kanye West
And his ramblings about Jewish people,
About how they are controlling everything,
From the media to the press to the banks,
And how he will do unspeakable acts,
Creating a platoon for eradication,
2020s United States turns into 1940s Germany.

I had to ask myself:
"Why die on this hill for this?
Why lose your career for this?
Why ruin your reputation for this?
Who hurt you? Who didn't give you love?
Who made you think the way you do?
Why, just why, and who, just who?"

I've known these people all my life,
I went to school with them,
I shared seats on the bus with them,
I went to work with them,
I shook hands with them,
I see them from all places in life.

And seeing his comments on a select few
To be broadened to the rest of the group,
Bring both sadness to my heart
And confusion to my mind,
That someone with his stature
Would promote this rhetoric, this idea,
This level of hate and destruction
As seen by dictators of the past,
And madmen of the present day.

But that's just the person he truly is,
Like it or not, that's the reality we live in,
So I guess we have to continue fighting,
His voice equals that of millions;
We are a small army with weakened weapons
Against his mighty force at his disposal.

But we should never back down,
Never surrender, never submit,
His words will haunt us for sure,
But will never scare us, frighten us;
And until he changes who he is now,
We will be ready at the frontline,
Defending those who cannot themselves.

Yesterday's Lost Time

Tomorrow will become today.
Today will become yesterday.
Yesterday will become forever lost.

Time on Earth is linear.
Unless we evolve to a higher plane,
We are all slaves to this fact,
Unable to break free, to overcome,
To go back and redo prior mistakes.

Only in the pages of a book,
Or the words spoken from old mouths,
Can we appreciate history in its purity,
But not through our own eyes,
Not through touch, sound, or taste,
We can't eat, can't hear, can't feel,
Our presence does not belong there,
Cannot relive alongside our ancestors,
Cannot share stories with one another,
Letting them die while we prosper,
With the cycle repeating itself further,
The generations after replacing us,
Left where we once took over the land,
Now buried alongside the previous owners.

I am afraid not of the unforeseen future,
But of the wastefulness of the present,
Which will turn to regret for the past.

Until the day we can travel back,
We have to continue moving forward,
And make memories worthy to remember,
Since this is a game we cannot escape from,
So, we must become players to the end,
Where we rest our heads once again,
And sleep for all of eternity;
Maybe then, we can hop between events freely,
Joining our bodies with those we couldn't before.

กรรมมีจริง*

When the man harassed the dogs,
And the pack vandalized his car,
All I can say is:
"กรรมมีจริง"

When the child was screaming,
Running around the restaurant,
And eventually tripped and fell,
Crying about their temporary injuries,
Crying for their parents to show up,
All I can say is:
"กรรมมีจริง"

When they threw stones at the monkey,
And it had no choice but to retaliate,
Flinging the rocks back at them,
Hitting one on the forehead,
Scattering all in every direction,
All I can say is:
"กรรมมีจริง"

When the woman stood her date up,
Did not appear when he needed her,
And then learned he has a lot of money,
A lot of fame, a lot of prestige,
Which he was hiding from everyone,
All I can say is:
"กรรมมีจริง"

When I am too full of myself,
Too high on arrogance, on vain impulses,
And someone gives me a reality check,
Put me where I should have belonged,
Gave me the tough advice I deserved,
All I can say is:
"กรรมมีจริง"

*กรรมมีจริง = "Karma is real."

Books by Prachatorn Joemjumroon:

Poetry:

A Fly On The Wall: Poems
Alternative Aggressor: Poems
Immorality Recorder: Poems
Moments In Time: Poems
Passing The Time: Poems

Stories:

Grim Reaper's Persuasion: Stories

Made in the USA
Coppell, TX
13 January 2023